BEHIND
THE
SCENES

A Guest Appearance

BEHIND THE THE SCENES

A Guest Appearance

Written by Jess Black

RANDOM HOUSE AUSTRALIA

A Random House book
Published by Random House Australia Pty Ltd
Level 3, 100 Pacific Highway, North Sydney NSW 2060
www.randomhouse.com.au

First published by Random House Australia in 2012

Addresses for companies within the Random House Group can be found at
www.randomhouse.com.au/offices.

National Library of Australia
Cataloguing-in-Publication Entry

Author: Irwin, Bindi, 1998–
Title: Bindi Behind the Scenes: A Guest Appearance /
Bindi Irwin, Jess Black
ISBN: 978 1 86471 842 3 (pbk.)
Series: Irwin, Bindi, 1998– Bindi behind the scenes; 3.
Target audience: For primary school age
Other authors/contributors: Black, Jess
Dewey number: A823.4

Cover photograph © Australia Zoo
Cover and internal design by Christabella Designs
Typeset by Midland Typesetters, Australia
Printed in Australia by Griffin Press, an accredited ISO AS/NZS 14001:2004
Environmental Management System printer

Random House Australia uses papers that are natural, renewable and
recyclable products and made from wood grown in sustainable forests.
The logging and manufacturing processes are expected to conform to the
environmental regulations of the country of origin.

Dear Diary,

When I went to Los Angeles to make a guest appearance on the hit TV drama *Riding High*, I thought the biggest challenge I would face was when the cameras were rolling. It turns out that what happened behind the scenes was where the real drama lay!

I discovered that all was not well on set and that the show was in jeopardy due to petty fighting and the inflated egos amongst the cast. From the outside, it looked as if they had everything anyone could want, but fame and money don't always buy happiness. This brings me to life lesson number three:

It's who you are and what you stand for that counts!

How do you keep your feet on the ground in Tinseltown? Good question! I realised during my week in Hollywood just how lucky I am to have good friends and family to keep me grounded and to help me out when times get tough. Otherwise, life can get pretty messy and confused. And, well, during my week away that's exactly what happened!

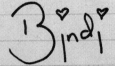

CHAPTER ONE

BINDI IRWIN SIZED UP A YOUNG

couple laden down with heavy backpacks as they

clomped past in sturdy hiking boots.

'My guess is they're jungle trekking in Borneo!'

Bindi whispered to her brother, Robert.

'Or backpacking in Nepal,' added Robert.

'Maybe they're going to Machu Picchu . . .' countered Bindi.

'Or perhaps he's an archaeologist heading to a dig!' exclaimed Robert.

Both of them looked around the busy terminal for more travellers to create stories about. Los Angeles International Airport was a hive of activity despite the early hour and it offered heaps of choice as travellers of all kinds bustled to and fro. Bindi and Robert loved to people watch and, having spent many hours in airports over the years, they had turned the game into a fine art.

Even though she'd just hopped off a long haul flight from Australia, Bindi felt refreshed and ready for adventure. She looked among the sea of faces milling about for others who gave off a similar vibe, and her attention was caught by three very excited young children careering through the terminal with their tired-looking parents in tow.

'Disneyland!' Bindi whispered, with a knowing smile.

'Too easy,' said Robert, looking around for another challenge.

'Come on, kids,' said Terri, as they stepped onto a travelator to speed up the long trek to the baggage-claim area. 'Someone from the studio is meeting us so we shouldn't keep them waiting.'

The family stood side by side and watched as their surroundings whizzed by in fast forward.

'I know!' cried Robert with a twinkle in his eye. 'A celebrity about to appear in a hit TV show about horses!'

Bindi looked around the terminal eagerly with thoughts of Taylor Swift or someone in country-and-western gear, but she couldn't find a famous face she recognised. 'Who?' Bindi asked, confused. 'Where?'

When nobody spoke Bindi realised her mother and Robert were looking at her and trying not to laugh. Then it dawned on her. 'Me!' Bindi exclaimed.

'Got you!' Robert laughed.

Bindi giggled and then felt a little self-conscious. 'It feels weird to hear myself described like that,' said Bindi. 'I would have got it first thing if you'd said Wildlife Warrior!' she added.

'We're very proud of you, darling,' said Terri, as she gave her daughter's shoulder a squeeze.

'Thanks, Mum!' said Bindi. 'I've been looking forward to this week for ages!'

Three months before, Bindi had read for a guest

role in an episode of the tween drama series *Riding High*, which was based in LA. A fictional one-hour drama, it revolved around three teenagers who kept their horses at the exclusive LA Riding High Equestrian Centre. To sum up the show's appeal and success, it was like *Victorious* on horseback, and Bindi couldn't wait to join the action!

'Will this travelator ever end?' asked Robert, craning his neck. He was itching to use his legs again. Fourteen hours in the air was like mandatory time-off, with no phone communication and lots of time for great movies, snacks and a bit of sleep. Robert was now ready to move on to their next adventure.

'Perfect timing – there's the exit!' said Bindi, pointing to a sign up ahead for baggage collection. She was also eager for them to get going. Bindi was really looking forward to meeting the cast and crew, not to mention the horses, of the show.

The Irwins hopped off the travelator and headed to their carousel to collect their gear. Another favourite game of Bindi and Robert's was to try and match travellers to their bags. They sure had made an art out of passing time in airports! Robert won the game two out of three by picking a pink Dora bag for a cute little three-year-old girl standing near them. After they retrieved the third and last bag, they made their way out through the main arrivals foyer.

'Ah, here's our ride,' said Terri, as they navigated their way through the crowd. She pointed to a well-dressed woman holding up a sign which read 'Welcome, Bindi Irwin!'.

'Cool!' exclaimed Bindi. 'I've always wanted to

be met by a sign with my name on it!' Terri and Steve had experienced this many times before but this was a first for Bindi.

The Irwins waved, and the woman with the sign smiled brightly and quickly made her way over to them. She was immaculately dressed in a black business suit with long pants and black patent stilettos. Her blonde hair was pulled back into a slick ponytail, and she wore bright pink lipstick.

'I'm Alison Foveaux, PR representative for NCN Studios,' she said brightly, before shaking each of their hands in turn. 'Welcome to LA!'

'Thanks, Alison!' said Bindi, beaming with excitement. 'It's good to be here.'

'Thanks for meeting us,' added Terri.

Alison peered at the small bag which each of

the Irwins carried. 'Is *that* everything?' she said, looking confused and slightly incredulous.

Robert grinned. 'We travel pretty light.'

'You sure do – I'd need a bag that size just for my *shoes*!' exclaimed Alison, with a laugh. She motioned for the Irwins to follow her through the crowd. 'We have a car waiting for you out front.'

As they threaded their way through the throng of people and out into the warm air, Bindi felt a sudden jolt of excitement. In less than an hour she would be at NCN's main studio meeting the director of *Riding High*. She had read for the role remotely, and although she had met Brad the director via Skype, they were yet to meet in person.

As Alison led them past a long line of taxis, Bindi noticed a silver limousine parked at the head of the taxi queue. It was an instant reminder that they were no longer at her home in Beerwah, Queensland! This was Los Angeles, where lots of famous movie stars and personalities travelled in style. She met Robert's eye. They were both thinking the same thing. Who was the traveller who would be using the car and where were they going?

'Your car awaits you,' said Alison, motioning towards the glistening silver Cadillac. Bindi realised the traveller using the limo was her!

'That's some car,' she said.

'Awesome!' Robert cried. He loved cars and was quick to jump inside as the uniformed chauffeur held the door open for them.

Alison laughed. 'We like to make our guest stars feel special. After all, this is LA!'

'It sure is!' exclaimed Bindi, as she piled in after her brother. Now that she had arrived, Bindi realised the time for playing games was over. Being in LA wasn't just for fun – it was beginning to feel very real.

CHAPTER TWO

THE LIMOUSINE WAS AMAZINGLY

quiet and comfortable, not like a real car at all. It hardly felt as if they were moving, let alone negotiating the busy LA traffic. And the inside of the Cadillac was as impressive as the exterior. It was kitted out with everything high-tech you could possibly imagine, much to Robert's delight. There was even a fridge for drinks as well as a snack bar.

Terri sat back with a sigh. 'This is heaven after fourteen hours cramped up in economy.'

'You got that right!' exclaimed Robert, busy fiddling with a remote control he'd found.

Alison smiled, pleased that they were comfortable, and turned her attention to Bindi. 'Brad won't keep you long, Bindi, so you'll soon be able to settle in at the hotel and get some rest.'

Bindi nodded, though she didn't feel tired at all. There was far too much adrenaline and excitement coursing through her body.

Alison noticed Robert eyeing the drinks cabinet. 'Can I offer you some refreshments?'

All three Irwins nodded. A cool drink sounded perfect. Alison handed Robert and Bindi a juice each and passed Terri a can of lemonade, then turned her attention to the iPhone that had been buzzing and flashing in her lap since they entered the car. 'Excuse me, duty calls.'

Bindi was happy to sit back and take in the city as Alison typed busily on her phone. Her fingers were moving so fast, they were almost a blur. Everything about Alison seemed flawless. Not only was Alison expensively dressed but Bindi noticed that the interior of the car now smelled strongly of her perfume. Her hair and make-up were immaculate, and when she smiled, her teeth were dead straight and dazzlingly white.

Satisfied that she had seen to all her emails, Alison placed her phone down and turned her full attention to Bindi. 'We're really very excited to have you on board,' Alison said with a smile.

'The director was *so* impressed with your read and is looking forward to working with you.'

'Thanks!' said Bindi. She was excited to meet Brad and, despite the words of encouragement from Alison, could feel that she was a little nervous.

'And I'm sure you'll have lots of fun on the show – all the kids seem to,' Alison continued in her bubbly voice. 'Our main cast are very experienced and everyone on the show is just such good friends. We're one big happy family really.'

Alison flashed her perfect teeth again and, after glancing out the window, checked her watch. Not satisfied with the progress they were making, she leaned forward to give instructions to the driver.

Bindi gazed out the window and noticed that they were off the main freeway and were now making their way through the suburbs. It looked like a very affluent part of town as the houses were *enormous*. The sky was clear and blue and the wide roads were dotted with tall palm trees.

'What was I saying before?' asked Alison, as she settled back into her seat and smoothed out the imaginary creases in her trousers. It was hard to picture Alison ever looking flustered or messy. 'That's right, I was saying that Savannah, Taylor and Andrew are just the best of friends,' she continued. 'They've been inseparable since the show started.'

'I can't wait to meet them!' said Bindi. She knew well enough not to make assumptions about people but she couldn't help but wonder if the actors were anything like the characters they played. It would be interesting to find out!

Alison glanced down at her phone as it beeped, then looked up at them apologetically. 'Excuse me, again, I just need to check this message.'

Robert had been doing a full visual inventory of the technology in the car and was now beginning to feel restless. He picked up a television remote which lay on the cabinet to the side of the car. 'Is it okay if I watch television?' he asked.

Alison looked up and nodded, with a smile. 'Sure, just hit the power switch on the remote.'

Robert did as she said, and from a corner of the car, a panel slid open with a *whoosh*. A sleek television screen popped out and lit up.

'Cool!' exclaimed Robert. He turned to Bindi and Terri. 'You've gotta admit *that* is cool!'

An entertainment show called *All the Hype* was on, and a presenter was talking animatedly about some Hollywood scandal. It took a few seconds for Bindi to realise they were talking about a cast member from *Riding High*.

'Let me see this,' said Alison, as she took the remote from Robert and turned up the volume. Her sparkling smile was soon replaced with pursed lips.

Terri and Bindi exchanged a glance.

'A series of tantrums, diva demands and late-night partying has plagued this once top-rating show currently in its third series. Rumours are flying that the network has had enough and, unless ratings improve, *Riding High* will be axed,' the presenter concluded dramatically, before moving on to another topic.

Alison switched off the television. The screen went black and, as if being chastised for the news it had brought them, quickly disappeared back behind its hidden panel. She gave an exasperated sigh but her expression remained composed. 'It looks like my day just got a little busier,' she managed to say brightly. 'These shows have no real news so they just make up rumours!'

If such a thing was possible, Alison's phone rang and beeped at the same time. Bindi imagined that Alison's inbox was filling up fast after that segment of *All the Hype.*

'Excuse me,' said Alison, raising her phone to her ear.

For the rest of the car ride, Alison took call after call. Bindi wondered how much truth there was behind the story, if any. She knew not to place much significance on what the popular media passed off as the truth, but judging from Alison's reaction, she couldn't help feeling that there may be a sliver of truth to the reports.

The car turned a corner and, for the first time, Bindi could see the huge white capital letters high up on the Santa Monica Mountains – HOLLYWOOD.

'Look, Mum,' Bindi pointed. Seeing that sign never ceased to give her a buzz of excitement.

Terri leaned over to get a better view and smiled at the sight. 'Yes, Hollywood . . . ' Terri ruffled her daughter's hair. 'Let the games begin!'

CHAPTER THREE

THE MAIN FOYER OF NCN STUDIOS

was everything Bindi had imagined it would be and more. In the style of old Hollywood, it had a marble tiled floor and rich cream walls adorned with framed awards and life-sized posters of cast members from their many successful TV shows.

A high ceiling featuring a glittering chandelier loomed above them, lighting up the main foyer and reception desk.

Alison's high heels made a click-clack sound which echoed as she walked briskly towards a young woman behind the reception desk. 'Hi, Madeleine. This is the lovely Bindi Irwin, here to have a meet and greet with Brad. And this is her mum, Terri, and her brother, Robert.'

'It's so exciting to meet you, Bindi!' gushed Madeleine as she shook Bindi's hand.

Alison turned back to the Irwins. 'I'm sorry to leave you here like this but I must dash. Madeleine will look after you. I'll be in touch to find out how your morning went.' She gave Bindi a kiss on the cheek. 'You'll be fantastic, Bindi, thanks again.'

'Thank you for all your help, Alison! I hope everything works out,' said Bindi.

They could hear Alison's phone ring as she turned to walk out. 'Hello? Yes, Barry, I saw it too. Of course there's no truth to those rumours. Our cast are true professionals . . .' Alison waved as she strode away, then gave a little laugh. 'Don't believe everything you see on TV, Barry, especially not from rival networks who are behind in the ratings!'

'I hate to think what her phone bill is every month,' commented Terri, as she and Robert took a seat on a couch beneath the chandelier. Bindi felt like she needed to stretch her legs after sitting on the plane for so long, so she thought she'd have a look around. She noticed Madeleine was reading a gossip magazine. Bindi could see a photograph of Taylor, one of the main actors from *Riding High*, on the front cover. This show certainly created lots of hype, that was for sure!

Madeleine looked to be in her early twenties and was dressed in a fitted pencil skirt with a black blouse and red heels. She looked every inch a movie star.

'You must get to meet all kinds of celebrities by working here,' said Bindi.

Madeleine nodded. 'It's one of the perks of the job!'

Bindi turned her attention to a life-sized poster of the girl from the magazine, which hung on the wall in front of her. 'That's Brooke from the show, isn't it?' Bindi asked Madeleine, as she pointed to the pretty girl with short auburn hair and freckles.

Madeleine nodded encouragingly. 'Her name

is Taylor Sanderson. Right now on the show, Brooke has just told Dean that she really likes him.' Madeleine shook her head sadly. 'But he says he can only think of her as a friend or a sister. It's totally tragic. As you can imagine, she's shattered.'

'I know,' said Bindi. 'We're behind in Australia, but Brad sent me some DVDs to catch up.'

Riding High centred around three main characters, Cindy, Brooke and Dean, good friends who shared a love of horses. But this friendship was complicated by the fact that Dean liked Cindy (who wasn't interested in him) and Brooke was in love with Dean (who didn't see her in that way). It was this love triangle set around competitions, Pony Club, and the day in, day out of looking after horses, which had made the show such a hit.

'And then *your* character, Eden, comes along!' continued Madeleine. 'She's going to make Cindy and Brooke so mad because they'll worry that Dean likes Eden,' she laughed. 'You have to excuse me for babbling, Bindi. I'm a huge fan of the show so I live and breathe it!'

Bindi laughed. 'I noticed Taylor was on the cover of the magazine you were reading.'

'Oh that,' Madeleine grabbed the magazine and held it out with disdain. 'It's ridiculous. They pick on Taylor because of her family being so famous and wealthy.' She leaned in closer to Bindi and lowered her voice conspiratorially, 'Her dad owns Blue Skies, the airline.'

Bindi nodded – she remembered she had read that somewhere.

'And her mum is, like, her agent,' continued

Madeleine. 'Mrs Sanderson's in here *all* the time. I'm kind of hoping she might be my agent too – I'm trying to break into acting as well. This,' she gestured to the foyer, 'is just my day job.'

'Good for you,' said Bindi. 'I'm sure you'll land a gig in no time.'

Bindi was reminded that almost everyone in LA was aspiring to work in the entertainment industry. 'And that's the actress that plays Cindy?' She pointed to a poster of another pretty girl who had long straight blonde hair and, in contrast to Taylor's pale skin, was tanned.

Madeleine turned to look at the poster and nodded. 'Uhuh, that's Savannah Atwood.'

Bindi walked over to take a closer look. She followed the series of press clippings along the wall below Savannah's poster, as well as the

TV stills which featured the actress over the last three series. Bindi was surprised by what they revealed. They charted a progressive change in Savannah's outward appearance. Not only had she lost weight over the years, but she increasingly wore more make-up and dressed more provocatively.

'And that's Andy,' Madeleine said, pointing to a poster of a really cute guy, who looked a little older than the girls. He had sandy blond hair that flopped over one side of his face, blue eyes and a big grin. 'Andrew Devine plays Dean on the show,' she explained, then, after a pause, added, 'He's a really nice guy *and* really cute!'

Before Bindi could agree, the switchboard rang, and Madeleine excused herself to take the call.

Terri checked in with Bindi, 'You ready, honey?'

Bindi nodded. 'Ready as I'll ever be.'

They were suddenly joined by a young man carrying a clipboard and looking short on time. His cheeks were flushed and he glanced quickly at his watch before speaking. Bindi couldn't help but notice that everyone in LA seemed to be ruled by their watches.

'Bindi!' he exclaimed, while shaking her hand enthusiastically. 'I'm Stuart, the show's runner, nice to meet you. It's my job to look after you during your time here at NCN Studios and get you from A to B.'

'Hi, Stuart,' said Bindi brightly.

Stuart gave Terri and Robert a wave. 'Such an honour to meet the Irwins,' he said, as his words tumbled out in a rush. He checked his watch again. 'We're running to schedule for once,' he said, sounding almost surprised. 'Bindi, would you mind coming with me to meet Brad?'

Bindi smiled. 'Sure thing.' She turned to her mum and brother. 'See you guys later then?'

Terri nodded. 'We'll be resting at the hotel.' She gave Bindi a hug. 'Good luck, sweetheart, I know you'll be great.'

Robert gave Bindi a playful punch on the arm. 'See you later, alligator.'

It felt a little surreal to Bindi that this moment was finally happening. She gave them a final wave and hurried after Stuart, who was already moving at a rapid pace down the long corridor.

CHAPTER FOUR

STUART LED BINDI DOWN passage after passage past offices and conference rooms until finally they exited the building and stepped out into the warm air. The humidity made Bindi think of home, though at the same time, she felt a world away from the zoo and her animal friends.

'This is Brad's trailer,' Stuart announced, as he stepped up to knock on the door. Once they'd come to a stop, Bindi realised she was out of breath. Being a runner was good exercise!

A muffled voice called out for him to enter, so Stuart stuck his head inside. There was a brief exchange which Bindi couldn't hear, and then leaving the door ajar, Stuart turned back to her. 'Brad's just on a call right now but he'll be out in a minute.' Stuart pointed to a foldable chair outside the door. 'Can I get you anything while you wait?' He glanced at his clipboard, then checked his watch again.

'I'm fine thanks,' Bindi gave him a smile. 'You go do what you have to do, no need to worry about me.'

'You'll be great!' Stuart gave her a grateful smile as he jogged away. 'I'll catch you later!'

Bindi sat down and stared at the nameplate on the trailer door, which read 'Brad Owen, Director'. Bindi had done her homework and had googled Brad's career. He'd been a television director for many years and was well respected within the industry. Even film actors thought it was a coup to get to work with him in television.

'I'm telling you, David, you're overreacting. It's a small dip in the ratings, we'll bounce back. It's all cyclical.' Bindi could hear the director's voice through the crack in the door. 'Alison's onto it, don't worry about a thing.'

Bindi wondered just how much trouble *Riding High* was in. It was sounding less and less like a smash hit and more and more like a train smash.

Finally, Brad's voice went quiet and the door was flung open. Bindi looked up at the man looming in front of her. Her first impression of Brad Owen was that he was really tall! Bindi jumped up from her chair.

'Bindi Irwin!' Brad stooped to Bindi's height and vigorously shook her hand. 'Am I happy to see you!' He disappeared back inside the trailer, then popped his head back out. 'Come in, come in!' he beckoned with a smile.

In stark contrast to the grand foyer of NCN Studios, Brad's office looked like a disaster area. There was paperwork scattered everywhere, empty mugs of coffee and piles of scripts which looked set to topple at any moment. And Brad was about as dishevelled as his office, with long scraggly brown hair and a beard he played with constantly.

'Sit, sit,' he insisted, as he settled himself back into his office chair. His long legs seemed to take up the remainder of any free space in the cramped trailer.

Bindi looked down at the only other chair in the room, piled high with books. Brad noticed her hesitation and waved. 'Just plonk them on the floor.'

Something about his scatty yet welcoming manner made Bindi relax. Despite being a high-profile TV director, Brad Owen seemed like the kind of guy you could sit down with to have a chat.

'Today is just a formality,' he began. 'I want you to feel right at home so that Eden feels right at home.' He talked with his hands, and Bindi couldn't help but notice how huge they were. Bindi realised he was still talking and forced herself to concentrate.

'Just be your fresh-faced Aussie self,' he continued. 'Be exactly as you were in the reading.'

'Beauty!' said Bindi, feeling excited and relieved at the same time. That was definitely something she could do.

Brad laughed. 'And those Aussie expressions – keep them coming. We love them!'

'Bonza!' said Bindi, with a grin.

Brad chuckled as he began to rifle through the piles of paperwork on his desk. 'Here we go,' he said, pulling out what looked to be a worse-for-wear script. He thumbed through a few pages. 'So, Eden buys a new horse and she keeps it at Riding High until she can take him home. She meets the kids – Brooke, Cindy and Dean – and her presence makes the girls a little jealous.'

Bindi nodded. She knew her lines off by heart

and the episode back to front. She had almost driven her mum and brother crazy practising her lines over and over again.

'How about we have a read-through of some dialogue?' Brad asked.

'Sure thing,' said Bindi. She cleared her throat and sat up straight in her chair. Reading on camera was very different to being face-to-face with the director!

'Okay, I'll read the part of Dean in the scene when the two of you meet for the first time.' Brad's finger scanned the page to the right place. 'And I'll read the part of Cindy too. Shall I print a copy for you?'

'No thanks,' said Bindi. 'I know my lines.'

Brad nodded happily. 'Good to hear! Let's begin.'

Bindi closed her eyes and imagined she was riding her new horse for the first time. Then she envisioned her ride being interrupted by a good-looking guy with a cheeky grin, watching from the fence.

DEAN: So you're the Aussie who bought Jude. He's a top horse.

EDEN: I know! I've only owned him for about five minutes, but he's just the best!

DEAN: You're not so bad yourself. If you ever want to ride out with me, just say the word.

EDEN: Wow, that's really nice of you. Thanks!

Brad then read out the description of the action. 'Eden leads her horse back to the stables to unsaddle and groom him. As she's doing so Cindy approaches her. She may not like Dean in the way he wishes, but that doesn't mean she wants anyone else to have him.'

CINDY: Don't go getting too close to Dean – he's taken.

EDEN: I'm sorry?

CINDY: Did I stutter?

Brad began adlibbing and hamming up the part of Cindy, doing a great impersonation of a bratty Beverly Hills girl. Bindi had to concentrate really hard not to burst out laughing.

CINDY: What part of 'he's taken' didn't you understand, girlfriend?

Brad looked up from the script and laughed. 'I tell you, the girls can get so catty on the show. It's painful to watch!'

Bindi giggled.

Brad put down the script. 'I thought we'd read

this scene because I want you to think about a time in your life when you've had girls be less than friendly to you. The girls really put you through your paces – pardon the pun – in this episode. Have you ever had something like that happen?'

Bindi thought about the question before answering. 'I generally tend to get along with people. But that doesn't mean I haven't experienced people saying mean things about me.'

Brad leaned back in his chair with a thoughtful expression. 'And how have you dealt with it when people have said these mean things?'

Bindi took her time again. 'Um, I can't change what other people choose to think about me. I just try to be positive and keep going, I guess.' She shrugged and smiled.

Brad nodded, encouragingly. 'And that's *exactly*

what Eden does. She doesn't let these girls slow her down.'

Bindi thought she understood what Brad was driving at. 'So you're saying Eden doesn't get caught up in the hype that the other characters create?'

Brad clapped his hands together. 'I couldn't have said it better myself, Bindi! I think you'll be brilliant.' He put down the script and leaned forward. Adopting a very serious expression, he said, 'And promise me that you'll also have some fun!'

Bindi laughed, 'You betcha!'

Brad laughed too and stood up. 'Speaking of fun, how about we head down to the stables – there's someone I'd like you to meet!' He absentmindedly looked for his sunglasses, which were hidden under a notebook on his desk.

'Does this someone have four legs and a tail?' asked Bindi, her smile growing. She couldn't wait to meet her first co-star of *Riding High*.

'There's no getting past you Aussies, is there?' Brad chuckled, as he held the door open for her. 'Your steed awaits you, young Eden!'

CHAPTER FIVE

THE LA RIDING HIGH EQUESTRIAN

Centre was a school for those who lived around Beverly Hills, so it really was the *Victorious* for horse lovers. The stables used for the show had been custom-built at the studio. They were also the actual stables where the horses for the show were kept, which explained why the set looked so authentic. The fences were painted a glossy white, the stables were filled with fresh, clean-smelling hay and the horses looked as if they'd just stepped out of a day spa.

Brad pointed to a beautiful horse grazing in a nearby holding yard. 'That's Chestnut,' he said, fondly. 'He's the horse that Andrew rides.'

'Wow!' breathed Bindi. 'He's beautiful.' Bindi gazed in awe at the gelding. His coat shone a golden chestnut and looked brilliant in the sun. He looked to be fit and in excellent condition. His tail flicked lazily against his thigh as he grazed contentedly.

'Believe it or not, he has a stand-in,' said Brad. 'All the horses do. We can't afford to lose filming time if one of the horses is out of action, so they have doubles. Even our actors don't have doubles!'

'Nor do I,' said a female voice, coming from somewhere to their left.

'Gerri?' called Brad, with enthusiasm. 'Come and meet Bindi.'

A young woman's face popped up from one of the stalls.

'Hi there,' she said, with a welcoming smile and a spade in one hand. 'I'm always telling Brad that if I were ever to take a sick day he'd be in real trouble. I keep threatening to but I never do.' She wagged a finger at Brad, who laughed.

As Gerri approached, Bindi was able to get a better look at her. She had long blonde hair tied back in a casual knot and she wore black jodhpurs, worn leather boots and a blue T-shirt with a logo for horse food on it. What struck Bindi most about Gerri was how fit she looked and the way she carried herself. Her arms were muscular and her torso was lean, while her manner was friendly but also professional. She wasn't gushy in the way Alison was. Bindi instantly knew that she and Gerri were very alike – she reminded her of many of her zoo friends from home.

'We'd be lost without Gerri,' admitted Brad, with a smile. 'She's certainly the best trainer for camera I've ever had the pleasure of working with, that's for sure.'

'Aw shucks, Brad,' Gerri mumbled, gently nudging him in the ribs. Bindi could see there was real affection between the two of them. 'Jude is just back here. I'll lead him out for you,' said Gerri, as she ducked into another stall.

If Bindi had thought Chestnut was a good-looking horse then Jude was a supermodel. He was jet black and, like the other horses she had seen so far, was groomed to perfection. He had an inquisitive gaze, gentle eyes and a lively step.

'Bindi, meet Jude,' said Gerri. She watched the young Australian take in the horse with a mixture of awe and delight. Jude's ears flicked back and forth as he waited patiently.

'Hey, Jude,' said Bindi, as she stroked his neck. Jude turned his head towards her, and Bindi held out her open palm for him to smell. He gave her a welcoming snuffle.

'Are you guys seriously going to let me ride him?' asked Bindi.

'Right now, if you're up for it!' said Brad,

throwing a questioning look to Gerri, who nodded her agreement.

'Am I ever!' blurted Bindi. She couldn't wait to tell her mum and Robert!

'Here, hold him for me while I grab a saddle and bridle.' Gerri handed the rope halter to Bindi and disappeared into the tack room. With the efficiency of a seasoned professional, she quickly saddled Jude and slid the halter from his neck to put on his bridle. Gerri found a helmet for Bindi and, all at once, they were heading out to the nearby arena.

'I'll keep the rope attached until you feel comfortable,' Gerri said, holding on to the rope halter. She handed the reins to Bindi with an encouraging smile.

Gerri led Jude and Bindi into an exercise ring while Brad perched on the railing to watch. Bindi focussed on adjusting to Jude's long stride. She wanted to make a good first impression on Brad and Gerri. After walking around the ring a few times, she began to relax. Jude was very responsive – his gait was smooth and he was very comfortable to ride.

'Okay to leave you two to get better acquainted?' asked Gerri.

Bindi nodded, and Gerri unclipped the rope and walked over to sit with Brad. Bindi took a deep breath. 'Come on, Jude, let's see what you've got!'

She gave him a gentle squeeze, and he broke into a trot. It was soon obvious that he was a very well-trained horse and Bindi wasn't going to have to do very much! She felt comfortable enough to break into a canter and was beginning to really enjoy herself. She broke into a smile and looked up to see both Brad and Gerri giving her the thumbs up.

'Go, Jude!' Bindi spoke quietly to him as they made their way around the ring.

Deep in concentration, it was only her and Jude and the rush of the warm air on her face as they cantered along. Bindi was truly content when she was connecting with an animal, and this was felt even more deeply when she was horse riding.

As she rounded the ring again, Bindi looked up to see Brad waving an arm at something in the distance. Before she could think about why he was doing that, she saw a flash of bright yellow out of the corner of her eye. Jude saw it too and took fright. He shied and abruptly threw his weight to one side to get away from the foreign object which spooked him.

'Whoa there!' Bindi tried to calm Jude and regain control.

But Jude was too far gone. He bolted to the other side of the arena, and Bindi realised he was heading for the gate. If he jumped it, there was no way she would stay on. Hunched forward over Jude's neck, Bindi had already lost one stirrup and had completely lost her balance.

She held onto Jude's mane with all her might as he veered completely out of control towards the closed gate.

CHAPTER SIX

BINDI CLUNG ON TO JUDE'S mane, gripped her thighs as tightly as she could to the saddle and hung on with grim determination.

All but one watched on in horror. Luckily, Gerri knew the horse well and placed herself squarely in front of the gate. Jude swerved to miss the trainer and, as he gradually came to a trot, he seemed to finally run out of steam. Bindi was able to find the stirrups again and regain her balance. Once she had command of the reins, Jude immediately slowed to a walk.

'Steady there, Jude,' Bindi whispered soothingly, stroking his neck.

'You did well to stay on,' praised Gerri as she ran over. She took the reins, and Bindi dismounted. 'Are you okay?'

'I'm fine,' said Bindi, still a little shaken. 'I think Jude saw something which spooked him.'

'You don't say,' muttered Gerri, as she turned to look at Brad in the distance. Bindi followed her gaze. Brad was talking animatedly with the brightly clad figure. By the sounds of things, they were arguing.

'Come on,' continued Gerri, 'time to meet another one of your co-stars.'

Dressed in a jumpsuit so brightly coloured that it hurt Bindi's eyes, Savannah Atwood was hard to miss.

'You should know better than to wear fluorescent clothing down at the stables.' Bindi could hear Brad chastise the girl. 'And you should know not to make loud noises or hasty movements! You scared Jude, and Bindi could have been seriously hurt!'

The girl glared at Brad indignantly. 'Sheesh! I thought these horses were meant to be well trained!' She turned to stare at Bindi and Jude before adding, 'If the rider can't handle the horse, they have no business being here, right?'

Brad looked set to explode. 'Get changed out of this ridiculous outfit and see me in my office.'

The girl tossed her hair defiantly. 'Just because you have no appreciation for fashion doesn't mean you should judge me. This is the new season's colour blocking, it's *so* on trend.' She rolled her eyes. 'Fluorescent? I don't think so.'

Brad shook his head – he didn't look pleased at all. 'Save the sarcasm for when the cameras are rolling!'

Gerri suppressed a smile and gave the girl a wave. 'Hi, Savannah,' said Gerri. 'This is Bindi Irwin, she'll be our guest star for the next week.'

'Hi!' Bindi said brightly, although she was beginning to feel a little uncomfortable about Savannah's manner.

Savannah gave Bindi a weak smile and seemed more interested in appraising Bindi's outfit. Judging by her expression, Savannah was less than impressed. Bindi glanced down and saw that her jeans and top were now covered in horse hair and streaked with dirt and sweat. 'See you on set, Beedy,' Savannah said dismissively.

'It's Bindi,' Gerri corrected her, with irritation.

'Whatever!' said Savannah, as she turned away.

Brad turned wearily to Bindi. 'I'm sorry about that. How are you? We're lucky you didn't get hurt!'

'I'm okay, just a bit rattled,' Bindi reassured him. 'It's definitely been a memorable day on set!'

Brad smiled. 'You're a trooper. I'm going to have to spend some time with Savannah. Will you be okay if I leave you here?'

Bindi nodded. 'I'll be fine. See you tomorrow!'

Brad gave Gerri a wave and walked after Savannah.

Gerri raised an eyebrow and turned to Bindi. 'It's hard to believe that three years ago Savannah was as excited to be here as you are.'

'She sure has attitude,' agreed Bindi. They could still hear her high-pitched voice as she listed a string of complaints to her long-suffering director.

'Personally, I reckon she's just really insecure,' Gerri said.

Jude nudged his trainer's elbow and snuffled. 'All right, let's get you unsaddled and fed, mister!' She gave Jude a pat.

Bindi walked with Gerri and Jude back to the stalls. She helped Gerri give Jude a rub-down and, once he was settled back in his stall, Bindi helped Gerri with a few light chores. They refilled all the water buckets, and as they made their way from stall to stall, Gerri introduced Bindi to her equine charges.

Bindi inhaled deeply. The smell of horses and their feed was one of her fondest scents in the world. She let out a yawn and realised her jet lag was finally catching up with her.

'Time for bed,' announced Gerri, as she placed a call for Stuart to collect Bindi.

'I'm fine,' protested Bindi, as she tried to stifle another yawn.

Gerri shook her head. 'As your trainer, I insist you head back to your hotel, order room service and get some sleep!'

As much as she was enjoying her time with Gerri, Bindi knew she was right. She had a week of early starts and long days ahead of her. Bindi's hotel bed suddenly seemed very appealing.

CHAPTER SEVEN

BRIGHT AND EARLY THE NEXT morning, Bindi accompanied Stuart to the green room where she would wait until they needed her in make-up. It was a large lounge room casually furnished with couches, a stereo, a TV and a small kitchenette. Despite having been up since

5 am, Bindi felt refreshed and ready for the day ahead!

A young teenage girl and boy were already seated on a couch, both studying the day's scripts. Bindi immediately recognised them both as Andrew and Taylor, the two other main cast members.

Stuart introduced Bindi and, in stark contrast to Savannah's manner the previous day, they were both very welcoming.

'G'day!' said Bindi brightly.

Taylor smiled. 'Nice to meet you, Bindi.'

Andrew hopped up from the couch and shook her hand. 'Hey, Bindi! Welcome!'

A familiar face appeared in the doorway. Savannah was wearing another outlandish outfit. She wore silver sequinned leggings with a hot pink crop top and brown leather roman sandals.

Andrew gestured to the pretty girl. 'This is Savannah.'

Bindi nodded with a smile.

'We've already met,' said Savannah, as she brushed past Bindi and draped her long limbs over the couch with a sigh. 'I'm *so* over today already.' Savannah studied her nails that were long like talons and painted the same hot pink as her top.

Andrew busied himself making coffee, and Taylor went back to reading her lines.

Meanwhile, Stuart checked his watch. 'I'll go see if make-up is ready for you, Bindi. Be right back,' he promised and hurried out. He almost collided with Madeleine, who entered carrying three large packages.

'Delivery from Jackson St!' she crooned with excitement. Madeleine handed a parcel to each of the three girls and watched enviously as Savannah began to tear the wrapping open.

'Awesome!' Savannah cried. She pulled out a large shoulder bag from the parcel and draped it over one shoulder. 'I've been dying to get one of these!'

Bindi slowly unwrapped her package with a sense of dread. She had been given the same cream leather bag with gold detail. 'It looks as if it's made of snakeskin,' said Bindi.

'It is!' exclaimed Savannah. She was now posing in front of a full-length mirror. 'This is worth so much money!'

'Why have I been given a snakeskin bag?' asked Bindi, confused.

Taylor pulled out her bag. All three of them had been given the same kind.

'It's free marketing for fashion labels if they can get us to wear their clothes,' Taylor explained. 'Jackson St is a brand Savannah likes, so they keep her coming back by sending her free clothes and accessories.'

Bindi was unsure what to do with the offending item and gingerly placed the bag on the table in the middle of the room.

Taylor looked at Bindi's expression with amusement. 'I agree with you, it's pretty tacky.'

Savannah paused midway through preening. 'You don't know what you're talking about. This bag is totally hot right now!'

Taylor shrugged. 'It's not really my taste.'

Savannah swung around in excitement and pounced on Taylor's bag. 'So give me yours then. I know plenty of people who would kill for it!'

'People already have,' said Bindi.

Savannah glanced at Bindi, taken aback. 'What did you say?'

'Innocent reptiles died so that you could have this bag,' continued Bindi. She could feel the colour rising in her face.

Andrew cleared his throat and suppressed a smile as he sipped his coffee.

'It's just a couple of snakes,' Savannah hissed.

'It's not a couple,' argued Bindi. 'It's millions of snakes. It's a multimillion-dollar industry.'

Savannah chuckled nervously, clearly uncomfortable about the direction in which the conversation was heading. 'Nobody even likes snakes.' She looked to the others for support, but Andrew ignored her and Taylor didn't smile.

'*I* do,' said Bindi. 'The reptile species you see

in the shops today will be on the endangered list tomorrow.'

Savannah dismissively waved a hand in Bindi's direction. 'Look, Beedy, I don't think you've got your facts straight. Jackson St wouldn't do anything unethical. They're, like, fashion gods.'

Bindi took a deep breath. 'My name is Bindi, and plenty of fashion houses turn a blind eye to where their products come from or how they are made. Skin shed by snakes is too thin for bags, so the snakeskin you see in shops has come from snakes who are deliberately *killed* for their skin. There's nothing beautiful about it. Larger captured snakes are often first starved to loosen their skin and then stretched by being forcibly pumped with water. Snakes are routinely nailed to a tree and skinned alive, their bodies thrown on to heaps where they can take two days to die. It's horrific.'

Taylor looked ill. 'I didn't know that.'

Bindi nodded. 'I like to dress up and look as pretty as the next girl but –'

'I seriously doubt that!' Savannah quipped.

Bindi ignored her and continued, 'But when I see reptile products being used in fashion, all I see is death.'

Savannah stroked the bumpy leather bag. 'But snakeskin is so soft and beautiful,' she said pitifully.

'It is, I agree,' said Bindi. 'But it looked a lot more beautiful on the snake.' Bindi handed her bag back to Madeleine. 'Can you please return mine?'

There was a shocked silence as Madeleine slowly took the bag.

'You can't be serious?' said Savannah, as she gripped her bag tightly to her chest.

'I am,' said Bindi.

'I don't see how me having one little bag is going to make a difference to stopping the illegal trade in animal products,' said Savannah, a hint of desperation in her voice.

'It's about making personal choices,' said Bindi. 'If everyone who loved fashion decided not to buy this bag because it was made from snakeskin, don't you think that would send a message to Jackson St?'

Savannah rolled her eyes. 'Blah, blah, blah.'

Taylor handed her bag to Madeleine. 'Bindi's right,' she said. 'Can you return mine too, please?'

All eyes in the room turned to Savannah.

With her Jackson St bag securely on her shoulder,

Savannah hurried to the door. 'I just remembered I have to be in make-up!'

She was out the door so fast nobody had a chance to argue.

Andrew laughed. 'I haven't seen Savannah move that fast since, well, forever!' He turned to Bindi with a big smile. 'I have a feeling that, with you here, the next week is going to be very interesting!'

Bindi had a feeling Andrew was right.

CHAPTER EIGHT

A SHORT TIME LATER, DRESSED
as Eden in a pair of new black jodhpurs, a white silk
blouse and a pair of knee-high black leather riding
boots, Bindi found herself in the make-up chair.

Wendy, the head make-up artist, was dabbing
away at her cheeks, applying a layer of foundation

to her face. Bindi watched her reflection in the mirror as Wendy then dusted her with powder.

'Voilà! You look great,' said Wendy. 'Just hold still a little longer while I work my magic.'

Bindi obliged. It gave her a chance to close her eyes and breathe deeply. She felt ready for the scene, and being transformed into Eden before her very eyes helped her even more to get into character.

'Taylor, are you listening to me?' a shrill voice called out, piercing Bindi's thoughts.

Bindi opened her eyes. Through the mirror, she could see Taylor and someone Bindi assumed was Taylor's mother in the costume area at the opposite end of the trailer.

'Shh!' said Taylor, trying to keep her voice to a whisper. Taylor was getting dressed into her riding gear while her mum hovered nearby, obviously agitated about something.

'It's just not good enough, Taylor! I want Brad to keep you in centre frame at all times,' said Mrs Sanderson, as she held out a shirt for her daughter to put on.

Taylor frowned and dropped her gaze. She concentrated on doing up the buttons of her blouse and hoped her mother would drop the subject.

'I'll talk to him if you won't!' her mother threatened, and began to pace anxiously.

Taylor coloured as she glanced briefly at Bindi and Wendy. She cleared her throat and spoke quietly to her mother. 'Mum, we can talk about this later. I'm sure Brad knows what he's doing.'

Her mother gave a deep sigh. 'Sometimes I think he forgets who you are – who *we* are,' she added with emphasis.

'Mum,' Taylor pleaded, 'I need to get ready now and focus. Do you mind?'

Her mother took the hint and pulled her BlackBerry from inside a large shoulder bag. 'I have work to do anyway.'

Taylor watched her mum leave and then glanced over at Bindi. Their eyes met through the mirror, and Taylor gave an embarrassed shrug. Unable to talk because Wendy was applying lip gloss, Bindi gave Taylor a friendly wave.

'Ta da!' Wendy stood back and surveyed her work. 'What do you think?' She held up a mirror so that Bindi could see her new hairstyle. Wendy had whisked her shoulder-length hair into a complicated chignon bun. It looked magnificent. With a touch of subtle rouge and lip gloss, Bindi looked every inch a *Riding High* star.

'Wow!' exclaimed Bindi, impressed. 'Wendy, you've managed to turn a ponytail into a work of art.'

Wendy smiled, obviously pleased. 'Thanks, honey. Now skedaddle, I have a queue a mile long.' She waited for Bindi to hop down from the chair before calling out, 'Next!'

Bindi gathered her things together just as the intercom crackled to life. 'Bindi Irwin, five minutes to set. Bindi Irwin!'

Bindi took a deep breath to steel herself. She could do it!

Taylor held out her hand. 'I wanted to wish you luck, Bindi.'

'Thanks.' Bindi accepted the gesture, and they shook hands.

Taylor hesitated a minute, then asked shyly, 'Would you like me to walk you there?'

Bindi's eyes lit up. 'That would be tip-top terrific!' she exclaimed. Taylor laughed and Bindi knew she had just made a new friend.

CHAPTER NINE

THE HORSES' EXERCISE ARENA

was transformed. Gone was the peaceful atmosphere from the day before. Bright lights, sound equipment and cameras crowded the area, and the yard was packed with crew members setting up for the first shot of the day. Brad was seated behind a monitor discussing the shot with Sam, the cameraman. Spotting her, Brad gave Bindi a wave.

Bindi smiled and waved back, then looked around for Gerri. She found her giving Jude a last-minute going-over with a brush. Bindi instantly felt better knowing Gerri was there and walked over to join them.

'I think we're ready,' said Gerri, as she fussed over Jude's tack, making sure everything was tip-top.

'Thanks, Gerri,' smiled Bindi.

'You'll be awesome,' said Gerri, as she handed Jude's reins to Bindi. Jude was saddled and ready, and every inch of his coat and tack were gleaming. He let out a welcoming snort and seemed completely unfazed by the harried and noisy workers milling around him.

'Two minutes!' yelled the assistant director, a formidable woman named Lou.

It was time. Bindi put on her helmet and mounted her horse. She gave Gerri and Taylor a thumbs up and waited for Brad's direction.

Once he finished talking to the cameraman, Brad joined her. 'Hey, you certainly look the part and I know you'll be brilliant.' He gave Bindi a big smile before continuing. 'It's very simple. You ride Jude around the ring a few times, and when Andrew calls out to you, you halt Jude right at that mark.' He pointed to a spot marked with a white 'X'. 'Then you run your lines just like you did with me in the office yesterday.' Brad gave her a smile, 'You got that?'

Bindi nodded and cleared her throat. She just

wanted to get going now. The suspense was killing her!

'One minute!' yelled Lou, as she began to count down and cue Sam to get ready to shoot.

Wendy ducked over to Bindi, waving her brushes. Bindi obliged by leaning down so that Wendy could smooth a few stray pieces of hair and give Bindi's face one last powder.

'And . . . action!' called Lou, and Sam panned the camera to Bindi and Jude. There was no more time to think – Bindi heard her cue and sprang into action. She nudged Jude into a trot and began to ride around the ring. Out of the corner of her eye she could see the camera panning along a track parallel to them to keep her in shot. Everyone had gone quiet, and Bindi tried not to think about the fact that everyone's eyes were on her.

'Come on, Jude,' she whispered, as they trotted around the ring. She waited for Andrew's line, which was her cue to speak.

'Hi there!' said Andrew. He was sitting on the fence, watching her. Bindi looked at him and slowed Jude to a walk. She gave Andrew a smile and finally halted Jude just shy of her mark. She casually glanced at the cameraman, who gestured with his hand that it was okay and for them to continue.

'G'day!' she said in a chipper Aussie twang.

Andrew was completely in character as Dean. He looked supremely at ease, good looking and wealthy. He looked both Bindi and Jude over with appreciation. 'So you're the Aussie who bought Jude. He's a top horse.'

At that moment something changed in Bindi.

She became Eden. She forgot about the crew and the cameras, and just let the lines come to her naturally. 'I know! I've only owned him for about five minutes, but he's just the best!'

Andrew grinned. 'You're not so bad yourself.'

There was a pause. Dean was meant to ask Eden out for a ride. Instead, Andrew blushed, and Bindi noticed him falter. He was looking at something behind her, and all of sudden, the confidence of before melted away. He grew flustered and broke character.

'Cut!' yelled Lou.

Sam stopped filming, and Brad walked over to them.

'I . . . um . . .' Andrew looked at Bindi. 'Sorry,' he mumbled.

Bindi turned to see what Andrew had been

looking at. She couldn't say for sure but she thought Taylor was standing directly in Andrew's line of sight.

Andrew ran his hands through his hair, looking embarrassed. 'I completely blanked,' he said to Brad, shaking his head.

Brad ignored Andrew and gave Bindi a big smile. 'Bindi, that was just what I was hoping for. You have great projection and a natural presence – keep it up.' He turned to Andrew and his tone changed. 'You look beat, despite the make-up.'

Andrew shrugged. 'I just forgot a line. It won't happen again.'

Brad looked doubtful but let it go. 'Let's hope not.' He turned to the crew. 'Take two!'

The crew called out various commands to set up

for a reshoot. Bindi repeated her previous actions, trotting around with Jude until Andrew called out to her again. This time Bindi wasn't able to halt Jude in time and completely missed her mark. They had to start the shot all over again and, on the third take, were able to complete the scene. Bindi noticed that Andrew still seemed to struggle with his line to ask Eden out but finally managed to execute it to Brad's satisfaction.

'It's a wrap!' cried Lou.

'Well done, guys!' Brad called, from the monitor. 'Bindi, come over here and see for yourself.'

Gerri appeared by Bindi's side and took Jude's reins so that Bindi could view the playback. As she watched the monitor, she couldn't believe how different she looked. She was so dressed up and on such a well-groomed horse she appeared about fifteen years old! Bindi couldn't wait for her mum and Robert to see her transformation!

The next scene involved Brooke and Cindy watching Dean as he rode off with Eden. Bindi stayed and watched. It was great experience to see how the cast members transformed into the characters they knew so well. Quiet Taylor transformed herself into snobby Brooke but, as far as Bindi could tell, Savannah's Cindy wasn't that far removed from Savannah herself!

After the scene wrapped, Taylor approached Bindi. 'You were fantastic!' she said, and gave Bindi a warm hug.

Savannah raised an eyebrow. 'It's easy if all you have to do is trot around a ring. Wait until you actually have to ride on camera!'

Bindi was slightly stung by Savannah's attitude

but said nothing. She remembered Gerri's comment about Savannah being insecure.

'What's with you?' Andrew remarked, as he joined them. 'Can't you be nice to anyone?'

Savannah shrugged. 'Cool down – don't take your hangover out on me!'

Andrew looked incensed. 'I am *not* hungover!'

'Oh, come on, you look about a million years old on camera.' Savannah wagged a finger in front of his face. 'You need to think about getting some beauty sleep. If the show's eye candy isn't up to scratch, the fans will go elsewhere. Maybe you're the reason the ratings have dropped.'

Andrew shook his head, and Bindi noticed he looked to Taylor to see if she had anything to add, but she remained silent.

'Leave me alone, Savannah. You have no idea

what you're talking about,' Andrew warned, before walking away.

Savannah turned back to Bindi and Taylor and pouted sarcastically. 'He's so touchy these days, right?'

Taylor opened her mouth to say something but Mrs Sanderson appeared at her daughter's side, asking how the scene had gone. They fell into another strained conversation.

Savannah rolled her eyes and looked around with irritation. 'Where is Gerri?' she asked, holding out her horse, Arrow's, reins.

'I'll take him,' said Bindi, reaching for the reins. 'I have to return Jude anyway.'

'You don't have to, you know. It's their job,' Savannah retorted.

Bindi shrugged and smiled. 'I'm happy to do it.'

'You might have won everyone else over but your goody-two-shoes act doesn't wash with me,' Savannah huffed, giving Bindi a meaningful look. 'I've got my eye on you.'

She sauntered off, leaving Bindi completely lost for words.

CHAPTER TEN

WHEN GERRI SAW BINDI LEAD

Jude and Arrow into the main stable, she let out a cry. 'You didn't need to do that, Bindi! Someone should have called me.'

Gerri took the reins and tied each horse up to a nearby railing. 'I've got a lame mare back here – was just applying a poultice. The vet's on his way.'

'Is there anything I can do to help?' Bindi asked with concern.

Gerri looked at her with amusement. 'Are you trained as a vet, by any chance?'

Bindi shook her head. 'Although I help out at our wildlife hospital all the time.'

Gerri laughed. 'Australia Zoo better watch out, I'm going to hatch a plan to steal you away.' She handed Bindi a curry comb and pointed to Jude. 'Knock yourself out.'

They fell into a companionable silence as they worked at grooming the horses. The chaos of the set seemed a world away, and it was difficult to believe they were in the middle of a major network studio. The only sounds now audible were the horses' breathing, their hooves grating against the concrete and the sound of their tails flicking at flies.

'Have you been working on the show for long?' Bindi asked Gerri.

'Since the beginning,' Gerri replied, as she bent to scrape the dirt from Arrow's hoof with a hoof pick. 'It was different then,' she said, straightening up. 'I mean, it's been over three years now. A lot can change.'

'In what way?' asked Bindi. She was curious to know more about the cast and why there seemed to be so much antagonism between them. It seemed that the gossip surrounding *Riding High* wasn't all that far-fetched.

Gerri paused to think about the question. 'Andrew had never acted before. He was discovered by a talent scout at a gymkhana. He's a really good rider,' she said, then rolled her eyes. '*When* he rides.'

Bindi tried to picture Andrew before he became a star. She liked knowing that he was passionate about horses.

'What about Savannah?' Bindi continued, walking around Jude to brush his other side.

Gerri let out a laugh. 'Savannah was a country girl, if you can believe that! She was starry-eyed and humble in the beginning.' Gerri grimaced. 'Then she changed and it all became about how she looked and about staying in the public eye and all that garbage.'

Gerri picked up a day rug which was hanging from the railing and threw it over Arrow. 'LA is full of people like Savannah. It's really sad because if you had met her before, you two would actually have had heaps in common.'

Bindi found that hard to imagine.

Gerri buckled up the straps and straightened the rug so that it lay cleanly across Arrow's back. Satisfied, she turned back to Bindi. 'Are you going to ask about Taylor? I like her – we've always got along well. She's professional and polite . . . It's her family that I have a problem with.'

'How come?' asked Bindi.

'You've seen her mother hovering around her like a bad smell. Well, her dad's the complete opposite – he's never around. It's like they've forgotten how to be her parents. And in this industry you need people who can just be there for you.'

Bindi knew exactly what Gerri meant. She knew

all about the industry and how you needed a close family unit and good friends around you that you could trust.

'Maybe having you around will be good for them,' suggested Gerri. 'They've stopped listening to me, that's for sure. And they run rings around Brad.' Gerri checked her watch. 'I need to get going – I have a few other horses to bring in and get ready.' Gerri began packing away their brushes. 'Thanks for your all your help, Bindi. I wish more people around here were like you!'

'No problem at all, it was my pleasure. Doing this kinda stuff makes me feel more at home,' said Bindi, as she helped Gerri carry the gear over to the tack room.

Bindi thought about what Gerri had said. Maybe she could help Taylor, Savannah and Andrew just by being a friend to them. These guys needed her even if they didn't know it yet. She wondered if they had left for the day. As she mulled it over, Bindi suddenly had an idea.

'I've got to head off too! See you later, Gerri!' cried Bindi. 'Thanks!' She raced off towards the green room.

Gerri stuck her head out of the tack room. 'Thanks for what?' she asked.

But Bindi had already gone.

CHAPTER ELEVEN

BINDI ENTERED THE GREEN ROOM

to find Taylor and Andrew sitting on opposite ends

of the same couch. Andrew was reading a book,

and Taylor was learning her lines.

Savannah, on the other hand, was pacing

around the room while having a very animated

conversation on her phone. 'Way to go!' she suddenly squealed.

Savannah had changed out of her set clothes into a multi-coloured kaftan with sequin detail and white leggings. Her heels were staggeringly high and her nails were now painted a midnight blue.

'Let me know the minute you hear anything, right?!' Savannah cooed and put her phone into her bag with a flourish. Bindi noticed she was still using the snakeskin bag which Jackson St had given her. Bindi shuddered at the thought of what the snakes used to make it would have endured.

'What's going on?' asked Andrew. 'I can't concentrate on my book.'

'I have epic news,' announced Savannah, turning her million-dollar smile on the others. 'My agent has confirmed an appearance on *Take It to the Top*!'

'We're ecstatic for you, Savannah,' said Andrew drolly, before abruptly returning to his book.

'Congratulations,' said Taylor, quietly. 'It's really hard to get on that show.'

'Henry's really funny,' said Bindi. 'I thought I might wee my pants on national television!'

Savannah hadn't even noticed Bindi was in the room. '*You*'ve been on *Take It to the Top*?' she said with doubt.

'Yep, about four years ago,' said Bindi.

Savannah did the calculations in her head. 'So you would have been how old?'

'Nine years old,' said Bindi brightly. 'I was really nervous but he goes out of his way to make you feel at home.'

Savannah pouted and put her hands on her hips. 'Sorry, who are you again?'

'Duh!' said Andrew, giving up on his book and placing it face down on the couch. He leaned forward, articulating his words slowly and carefully as if speaking to a small child, 'She's B-i-n-d-i I-r-w-i-n!'

'You are such an idiot!' Savannah retorted. She was irritated by Andrew's patronising manner, but then nodded slowly. 'I remember now – you're the Crocodile Hunter's daughter, right?' She studied Bindi as the penny dropped. 'I remember . . . lots of khaki.'

Bindi giggled and nodded. You had to hand it to Savannah, she really did take notice of all things fashion related.

'Bindi's also been on *Oprah* and *Ellen*,' added Taylor, with a smile.

Savannah gasped, 'Oprah! She's, like, my hero!'

Bindi broke into a huge smile. 'Yeah, she's awesome. When she came to Australia she visited the zoo. Everyone loved her – even Agro the Croc, and he's a little on the grumpy side.'

Savannah eyed up the young Aussie. 'You have to tell me everything you know.'

'I wasn't on the shows for myself,' laughed Bindi. 'I was with my family and we were there to talk about Australia Zoo and promote the plight of endangered animals.'

Savannah gave her a dismissive wave. 'Yeah, yeah, plugging the khaki. I get it.' She looked intently at Bindi. 'Do you have like six pairs of those janitor uniforms or something?'

'Actually, you're not that far off the mark,' Bindi said, grinning. 'I have five.'

'Geez, why?' asked Savannah, looking horrified at the prospect.

'It's not just any khaki,' said Bindi, 'it's an Australia Zoo uniform. I am first and foremost an ambassador for the zoo and for Wildlife Warriors. Any success I have with acting helps to give me a platform on which to spread my message.'

Savannah began to lose interest. 'Right . . .' she said, turning back to study her nails.

Bindi pointed to Savannah's bag. 'You know the fashion houses try to defend their choices by saying they only use skins from farmed snakes, but there's a huge illegal industry. Something like 90 per cent of skins used in fashion are caught from the wild.'

Savannah threw up her hands in exasperation. 'Again with the bag! How did we get back on to this?' She pointed an accusatory finger at Bindi. 'You're obsessed!'

Bindi grew serious. She really wanted to get through to Savannah and help her see that her actions could have dire consequences. She took a deep breath. 'If caring about the welfare of innocent animals and reptiles makes me obsessed then I'm okay with that. My family and I have dedicated our lives to trying to curb the endangerment and extinction of animal species around the world.'

'What do you want – a medal?' asked Savannah sarcastically.

'I think it's great that Bindi believes in something,' Taylor piped up. 'She's looking at the bigger picture.'

Savannah rolled her eyes. 'Whatever,' she muttered, drawing out the syllables for emphasis.

Bindi refused to be deterred by Savannah's attitude. 'I appreciate that you're really into fashion, but you can still have a killer look without the killing.'

Savannah's pretty face crumpled into a frown. She wasn't used to being challenged like this.

'Savannah, what will you be talking about on *Take It to the Top*?' asked Andrew. 'Global warming, the European economy, or maybe how to apply a spray tan?'

'Play nice, Andrew,' said Taylor. 'It's great for Savannah that she'll be on *Take It to the Top*.'

'Thank you, Taylor,' said Savannah, sweetly. 'And just so you know,' she said tartly, turning to Andrew. 'I have all kinds of opinions about all sorts of things, if you took the trouble to ask.' She stared pointedly at him. 'Don't worry about me, it's *you*

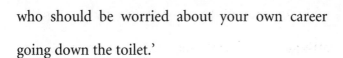

who should be worried about your own career going down the toilet.'

'Ouch!' said Andrew sarcastically. He slumped back onto the couch, theatrically clutching his chest as if Savannah had wounded him.

'Andrew, Savannah has a point,' said Taylor. 'We're all worried about you. The pictures of you in the magazines make you look like you're really out of control.'

Now Andrew looked genuinely wounded. 'You of all people can't talk about me being out of control!' he retorted. 'At least I have a life to do with what I choose.' He sat up. 'And I'm not out of control – I'm going out and having fun. You should try it sometime, instead of leading a life that's completely controlled by your mother!'

All of the colour drained from Taylor's

face. Bindi could see tears begin to well in her eyes.

Realising he had overstepped the mark, Andrew moved towards Taylor. 'I'm sorry, Tay. It's just, you only get one life. You need to start thinking about living it for yourself.'

'Leave me alone!' Taylor managed to blurt out before she burst into tears.

'Taylor . . .' said Andrew, reaching for her hand.

Taylor pulled away from him and ran from the room.

'Way to go!' Savannah snapped at Andrew. She stormed after Taylor as fast as her sky-high heels allowed.

Andrew groaned and flopped back onto the couch.

'Are you okay?' Bindi asked, worried.

Andrew sighed. 'I'll be fine, it's Taylor I'm worried about.'

Bindi had to admit that Andrew did look really tired. He had dark circles under his eyes and his once white-blond hair looked like it could do with a good wash.

He sat up again and looked at Bindi. 'Hey, can you do me a favour?' he asked quietly.

'Sure,' Bindi nodded.

'Can you go check on Taylor? She could really use a good friend right now.' He ran a hand through his hair. 'It doesn't look like I have that job anymore.'

Bindi really felt for him, he looked so sad. 'I'm sure you two will work things out,' she said, putting a hand on his shoulder.

'I'm not, but thanks,' Andrew said, before lying back on the couch and closing his eyes.

CHAPTER TWELVE

BINDI HEADED STRAIGHT FOR
the ladies' toilets. Sure enough, she found Taylor
washing her face at the sink while Savannah stood
awkwardly beside her.

'Hi,' said Bindi, hovering in the doorway. 'Am
I interrupting?'

Taylor looked up and dabbed her eyes with a tissue. 'Not at all,' she said, and gave Bindi a weak smile. 'I must look a mess.' She inspected her reflection in the mirror. Her fears were confirmed when she saw her bloodshot eyes, red cheeks and running mascara. 'The paparazzi will have a field day when they see this!' she groaned, as she ran more water over her face.

'Here,' said Savannah. She scratched around in her bag and pulled out a tube of concealer.

Taylor shot her a grateful look and began to apply the cream to her face.

'What do you say to us girls getting out of here?' asked Bindi, as she leaned against the wall and watched the other two in the mirror.

'Yes, please!' said Taylor. 'Far, far away!'

'What do you want to do?' mumbled Savannah, while retouching her lipstick.

Taylor shrugged. 'Anything that doesn't involve boys!' She looked as if she might start crying again.

'We could grab a juice?' suggested Bindi.

Savannah shook her head. 'No, girls. I have a much better idea!'

Bindi could hardly believe her eyes when their taxi pulled up at the exclusive shopping district of Rodeo Drive. She had heard about the three blocks of high-end shops and had seen it featured in movies, but she'd never visited it in person. For as far as she could see on both sides of the street was a long line of very expensive-looking boutiques.

Bindi felt like she was a world away from home and Australia Zoo, and marvelled at what different lives she and the girls led.

After Savannah had paid the taxi driver, she took an enormous pair of sunglasses from her bag and put them on. Taylor did the same and placed a black sailor's cap on her head, pulling it down low over her eyes.

Savannah noticed Bindi studying them with amusement. 'We have to go incognito when we're out in public,' she explained in a hushed voice.

Bindi nodded, trying to keep a straight face.

'I don't want to be recognised,' Savannah continued.

'And I look like a raccoon,' added Taylor, with a giggle.

The taxi driver adjusted his rear-view mirror

to get a better look at the passengers in the back seat.

'No autographs, please,' said Savannah, as she met his eye in the mirror.

Bindi couldn't take it anymore – she burst out laughing. 'What's so bad about being recognised?'

'All that chatting and fake smiling and auto-graph signing,' said Savannah. 'I can't stand it.'

'But people just want to meet you and congratulate you on your work,' said Bindi, still unconvinced.

'Maybe . . .' Savannah shrugged. 'Or maybe they want something from me. It's a jungle out there, you know.'

Savannah was a tough nut to crack. Bindi looked out of the window at the busy street full of shoppers. 'Do you think it's safe to get out now?' she teased, and turned to the others with a smirk on her face.

Savannah surveyed the landscape. 'Yes,' she said tersely, aware that she was being made fun of but not wanting to yield completely to the mockery. 'Just be on the alert, okay?'

Bindi hopped out of the taxi, followed by a more wary Savannah and Taylor. The street was bursting with shoppers but nobody paid them any attention. They stood in the middle of the pavement as Bindi took it all in. It was shop after shop of dazzling retail heaven down the famous street lined with palm trees. It was hard to know where to begin.

'Welcome to Rodeo Drive!' announced Savannah.

Bindi liked to shop like any girl her age but she had a feeling that Savannah would take the art of shopping to a whole new level. Still, it would be fun just to try on the beautiful clothes they had to offer!

As they walked, Bindi noticed a group of young girls who looked to be about ten years old walking towards them. She smiled at them, and one of the girls did a double take, letting out a squeal of excitement.

'We've been discovered,' whispered Savannah. 'Run for it!' She turned in the other direction and began to trot a little faster in her heels.

'NO WAY!' squealed the same girl, stopping right in front of them and blocking their way. She pulled a small notebook out of her diary and held it out. 'You're like my biggest hero!'

Savannah gave a sigh. The game was up. She turned to the girls with a fake smile.

'Bindi Irwin!' enthused another girl. 'You rock!' She held up her palm for a high five from Bindi. The young girls swarmed around Bindi, completely ignoring Taylor and Savannah.

'I've watched *Bindi the Jungle Girl* about a million times,' said a third girl, as she held out her diary for Bindi to sign. Bindi happily chatted to the girls, answering all the questions they threw at her, and gave them each her autograph.

Taylor and Savannah exchanged a glance. 'The girl guide makes it look almost . . . fun,' muttered Savannah, who was obviously put out at being sidelined.

After various high fives and hugs and poses for photographs, the girls finally calmed down. Bindi promised to email each of them before they finally continued on their way.

As a parting gesture, one very fashionably dressed tween turned to Savannah with a big smile and said, 'Great outfit by the way!'

Savannah brightened and looked visibly pleased. 'Thanks!' she said, and she meant it.

Once the girls had left, Bindi turned to her co-stars. 'That wasn't so bad, was it?'

'Er, surprisingly . . . no,' said Savannah. 'They were really nice.'

Bindi flashed Savannah a smile. 'So what are we waiting for? Let's go shopping!'

'*Finally!*' said Savannah and laughed.

CHAPTER THIRTEEN

'I'M BUSHED!' GROANED TAYLOR, as she slid into a booth.

After two very fun-filled hours of fashion, the girls had decided it was time to refuel. Savannah took them to a cute little café she knew and they chose a table by the window. For Bindi, it was fun just to watch the parade of fashionistas walk past in all their glory. After the waiter had taken their order, they sat back and relaxed.

'I have to thank you, Savannah,' said Bindi. 'The last few hours were a real education. I had no idea that I can pull off the colour watermelon.'

'Absolutely!' said Savannah earnestly. 'The brighter the colour on you, the better.'

Bindi wondered if her mum would agree with her sudden need to build on her wardrobe!

As if Terri's ears were burning, Bindi heard the familiar sound of her ringtone and reached for her phone. 'Hey Mum, how are you?'

Bindi listened as Terri filled her in on what she and Robert had been up to.

'Sounds like great fun! Us? Well, right now we're on Rodeo Drive if you can believe it! We tried on some clothes but nobody has bought anything . . . yet.' Bindi looked pointedly at Savannah. 'I'm not sure Savannah can hold out much longer, though!'

Savannah rolled her eyes and giggled.

'We'll probably be another hour or so. Shall I meet you guys back at the hotel?' said Bindi, and listened for Terri's response.

'Awesome, can't wait! Bye, Mum!'

Bindi placed her phone on the table.

'It sounds like you and your mum get along really well,' observed Taylor.

Bindi nodded and smiled. 'Yeah, my mum is one of my best friends.'

'You're lucky,' said Taylor, with a hint of sadness.

A waiter arrived with their milkshakes, served the old fashioned way in tall glasses with long straws. They each took a sip. Bindi had ordered chocolate and it was delicious!

Taylor pushed her strawberry milkshake to the side. 'I used to have a great time with my mum,' she said, 'until she became my agent.'

'What happened?' asked Bindi.

Taylor let out a long sigh. 'You can't say anything to anyone,' she said, then paused. When the others nodded, she continued, 'My dad travels heaps and he and Mum haven't been getting on very well lately. My sister has left for college and I work such long hours. My mum was so lonely . . . It was my idea she should manage me. I thought it would give her something to do, you know, get her out of the house.'

'Instead you created a monster,' said Savannah, as she took a long slurp through her straw.

Taylor's eyes flashed defensively, and Bindi sensed they were about to go back to their old pattern of arguing again. Surprisingly, Taylor agreed with Savannah.

'All we do is fight,' continued Taylor. 'And the worst thing is I can never get a break from her. She's at work *and* she's at home – she's driving me crazy!'

'I definitely get along much better with my mum since I put a few thousand miles between us,' agreed Savannah.

Taylor put her head in her hands. 'It gets worse.' She peeked out at the others through her fingers. 'Mum didn't think it was a good idea to date a co-star so she made sure my relationship with Andrew never really had a chance.'

'I wondered what happened between you two,' said Savannah.

Taylor's eyes filled with tears. She pulled out a tissue and dabbed at them. 'I can hardly talk to my mum anymore and I hurt Andrew so much . . . ' Her voice broke off with a sob. 'I don't know what to do.'

'Have you tried talking to your mum about how you feel?' asked Bindi, softly.

Taylor shook her head. 'I'm scared she'll fall apart if I take this job away from her.'

'As much as I hate to say it, Andrew is right,' said Savannah. 'Your mum will get over it and it's your life. If she's making you this miserable, you have to do something about it.'

Taylor reached for her milkshake again and twirled her straw. 'I'm not brave like you, Savannah.'

Savannah snorted into her drink. '*I'm* not brave!'

'Confident then, you're really confident,' Taylor corrected herself.

'Hmph, it's all an act,' Savannah said, with a wave of her hand, and sunk back into the booth.

'How do you mean?' asked Bindi.

'I grew up on a farm in Ohio!' snorted Savannah. 'I had about the best childhood any kid could have. Horses, animals, open spaces . . . then we lost the farm.' Her voice wavered but she steeled herself. 'We moved to a small town, Hicksville, south of nowhere. Not a horse in sight. This town had nothing going for it, right?'

'I never knew that,' said Taylor, with surprise.

'So what happened?' Bindi was intrigued to learn more about this other side to Savannah.

Savannah tossed her hair back. 'I don't know. *Riding High* was my ticket out of that place and

I am *never* going back.' She looked at the others defiantly. 'Do you two have any idea how much work goes into looking this good? I'll tell you one thing about being Savannah Atwood, it's exhausting.'

'But life shouldn't be like that,' said Bindi.

Savannah shrugged. 'Yet it is. There's always another Savannah waiting to take my place.'

Taylor looked at Savannah thoughtfully. 'You forget that I met you, the country bumpkin, fresh off the plane.'

Savannah blushed. 'You laughed at me, right?'

Taylor shook her head. 'Just the opposite. I really liked you. I thought we were going to be the best of friends.'

Savannah remained silent and looked out the window. The waiter arrived with their meals.

Nobody felt much like talking so they concentrated on eating the fresh salads in silence. Each lost in their own thoughts.

CHAPTER FOURTEEN

THOUGH IT WAS GETTING LATE,

Bindi found it difficult to get to sleep.

Her hotel bed was comfortable – check. She was tired – check. The room was quiet – check. Yet sleep wouldn't come. The cast and crew were heading out on location so they had to start extra early in the morning, but the more Bindi tried to sleep, the more restless she became.

Bindi decided to get up and make some hot chocolate. She and Robert were sharing a room in the hotel suite so she slipped out quietly, making sure not to disturb him. Once out in the lounge area, she realised she wasn't the only one who was still awake.

Terri looked up from her paperwork as Bindi walked in. 'Can't sleep?'

Bindi shook her head and plonked herself down at the table next to her mum. 'What are you doing?' she said, looking at the pile of papers surrounding Terri.

Terri sat back in her seat and stretched out the cramp in her neck. 'I'm working on a grant application for the wildlife hospital.'

Bindi looked at the amount of paperwork needed for just one application. She knew that the hospital struggled to make ends meet and only managed to stay open due to the dedicated service from volunteers. 'You look like you could do with some sleep,' she observed.

'I'm not the one with a 4 am call in the morning,' smiled Terri. She pushed the papers to one side. 'How about I make us both a hot chocolate?'

Bindi yawned. 'You read my mind.'

Terri poured some milk into a pot and put it on the stove in their little kitchenette. Then she walked over to Bindi and rubbed the back of her neck. When Bindi was a little girl and unable to sleep, her mum used to tickle her head and stroke her hair. It brought back so many memories. Bindi already felt the stress begin to ebb away. 'Thanks, Mum,' Bindi sighed, 'that feels great.'

Terri continued with her massage.

'I'm really lucky to have you as my mum,' whispered Bindi.

Terri paused. 'Thanks, sweetheart.' She brought her face around to meet her daughter's. 'Do you want to talk about it?'

'That obvious, huh?' laughed Bindi.

'I have known you all your life, you know,' teased Terri.

'I'm worried about my new friends on the show,' said Bindi. 'It's such a mess. They fight all the time and none of them are happy,' said Bindi, feeling herself becoming exasperated again.

'Fame and money don't guarantee happiness,' pointed out Terri.

The milk was threatening to boil so Terri poured it into two mugs and added a teaspoon of chocolate powder to each. Then she joined Bindi at the table.

'But I think they could be happy,' Bindi continued, taking her mug of hot chocolate. 'They just lost their way a little bit in la-la land.' La-la land was the Irwins' code word for the celebrity world – especially LA.

'It happens all the time. People think fame will bring them everything but it just tends to make life more complicated, unless you have a really strong goal.' Terri assessed her daughter as she sipped at her hot chocolate. 'You had to figure that out when you were very young.'

Bindi nodded thoughtfully. 'I had two terrific parents to guide me. It seems that not everyone is so lucky.'

Terri smiled and took a sip. 'Then you have to hope they have good friends like you who will remind them what it is that makes them happy.' She checked her watch. 'It's getting late and you have to be up very early.'

Bindi nodded and gave her mum a kiss. 'Thanks for the chat. I'll go to bed in a minute.'

'Okay, goodnight.' Terri whispered, as she left the room.

Bindi sipped her hot chocolate. She remembered an old exercise one of her teachers had taught her. It was a way of reminding yourself of the things that make you happy.

Bindi grabbed a piece of paper and made a list. She wrote down Savannah, Taylor and Andrew's names at the top of the piece of paper and drew a column between each name. Then she listed everything she knew that made each person happy. Once Bindi had written everything she could think of, she sat back and studied her list. One activity stood out as being something they all enjoyed.

Bindi tapped her pen on the table as she thought. She had an idea. It was pretty out there as ideas went but it might just work. She reached inside her bag and found her script for the next day, as well as the call sheet and contact numbers for all the *Riding High* cast and crew. She picked up her phone and dialled.

'Hello, Gerri?' Bindi asked, as she heard Gerri's sleepy voice on the other end of the line. 'Sorry if I woke you.' Bindi took a deep breath and plunged ahead. 'I've had an idea which might solve all of the problems on set and help Andrew, Taylor and Savannah as well. Thing is, I'm going to need your help . . . '

CHAPTER FIFTEEN

THE NEXT MORNING, THE ENTIRE

cast and crew of *Riding High* relocated to the

offsite location they regularly used for the action

sequence needed for each episode. The Los Angeles

Equestrian Centre and the adjoining Griffith Park

were situated close to the studios off Ventura

Freeway, and were the perfect venue for the cross-country event which occurred at the climax of Bindi's episode.

The crew had been setting up in the dark hours of early morning. By 5 am Bindi, Andrew, Taylor and Savannah were all seated in line for hair and make-up. The girls were clearly much more at ease in each other's company, but Bindi noticed that Andrew and Taylor were still not on speaking terms.

Brad approached and pulled up a chair opposite the four of them. He looked uncharacteristically downcast. 'Hi, team,' he said, as he ran his hands through his hair. He looked even more dishevelled than usual.

'Morning,' said Taylor, throwing Bindi a quizzical glance.

Savannah gave the director a smile.

Andrew looked up from his script. 'What's up?'

'I'll get straight to the point,' said the director. 'I've got some bad news.'

The others exchanged worried glances and waited for Brad to continue.

'Gerri's had an accident. She's okay but she's in hospital and can't ride for at least a week,' explained the director.

'That's terrible!' exclaimed Andrew.

'Poor Gerri!' said Taylor, suddenly looking concerned. 'Can we visit her?'

'Sure,' Brad nodded. 'I'll get Stuart to find out the details.'

'I feel for Gerri, of course, but the really bad news is for the show,' Brad said, grimacing, and shifted in his seat. 'We can't afford to close production while we wait for Gerri to get better. If we did, we'd be giving the studio the excuse they need to shut us down.'

'Surely the equestrian centre has heaps of stunt riders we could use?' suggested Savannah.

'They may do but they'll be expensive and Gerri had an exclusive contract with us. It would take a few days to sort out the legals and that also costs us time and money,' explained Brad, looking increasingly despondent.

Brad glanced at Bindi as he continued. 'I might as well fill you in now, Bindi. It's no secret that ratings have fallen and we're in trouble.'

'Surely there's something we can do,' said Bindi.

Brad shrugged and shook his head. 'Not really, my hands are tied.'

There was silence as the news sunk in for each of them.

'What if we do our own stunts?' suggested Bindi.

Brad paused, and Bindi noticed the smallest flicker of hope in his eyes. The actors all leaned forward, instantly interested in the idea.

'It's a ridiculous suggestion!' exclaimed Mrs Sanderson, who had been standing behind them, unnoticed. 'Not to mention irresponsible and foolhardy.'

'Sounds right up my alley then!' said Andrew, giving Taylor's mother a pointed look. He turned to the others with excitement. 'When you think about it, there aren't any big stunts. It's a simple cross-country event with a few jumps and a bit of racing. No big deal.'

Brad held up his hands for silence. 'Before we get too carried away here, Mrs Sanderson is right. There's a question of personal indemnity. Your agents would need to give approval and, of course, Gerri would have to sign off on it.'

'It's absolutely out of the question,' asserted Mrs Sanderson.

'Mum,' said Taylor, in a firm voice, 'I think Bindi's suggestion is a good one if it means saving the show. It's certainly worth considering if the stunts aren't dangerous and are something we all feel competent and confident doing.'

'Your mum's right, Taylor,' Brad jumped in, 'it's not a good idea.'

Mrs Sanderson crossed her arms triumphantly.

'At the end of the day, I'm the one doing the riding,' Taylor said to her mother. 'It's my decision.'

Andrew and Savannah exchanged looks. This was the first time they had witnessed Taylor stick up for herself during a disagreement with her mother.

'Next you'll be telling me you don't need my help,' Mrs Sanderson laughed.

'Mum . . .' Taylor began. She searched for the right words. 'It's *my* life. I appreciate everything you've done for me but I'd rather you weren't my manager anymore.'

There was a brief pause before Mrs Sanderson replied. 'I'm sorry, what did you just say to me?'

'I said that I no longer want you to manage me,' said Taylor, doing her best to keep her voice steady.

Mrs Sanderson crossed her arms and

harrumphed. 'You need a manager to look out for your best interests.'

Taylor took her mum by the hand. 'You're right, but I also need a mum.'

'I thought I was doing a good job at being both,' Mrs Sanderson huffed defensively.

'Well . . .' Taylor hesitated. 'I think they're both a full-time job and the managing takes so much out of you that I don't get to see my mum very much. And I miss her.'

Mrs Sanderson's eyes filled with tears. 'Oh, honey . . .'

Mother and daughter hugged while the others watched on. Savannah surreptitiously brushed a tear from her eye.

Andrew looked at her and winked.

'Mascara,' she muttered, as she rubbed her eyes.

Andrew gave her a wry smile but didn't take the opportunity to make fun of her. Instead, he handed her a handkerchief. Without saying a thing they both knew that, for once, they were on the same page.

'I know we all have to get our agents' approval but I think we should do it!' declared Andrew.

'So do I!' agreed Savannah firmly.

'This is a first for the record books,' chuckled Brad.

Andrew turned to Bindi. 'How about it?'

'I'm keen as mustard!' she cried, and then as an afterthought Bindi added, 'I'll have to check with my mum but I reckon she'd love the idea.'

'So what are we waiting for?' Savannah challenged Brad.

Brad's face lit up. 'You'll do it?'

'That's what we're here for, isn't it?' exclaimed Taylor, her cheeks flushed. 'To ride!'

'This isn't going to be easy,' said Brad, looking at Savannah with emphasis. 'It will be dirty work.'

Savannah held out her hand and flashed a huge sparkling ring on her middle finger in front of Brad's face. 'You know what they say, pressure makes diamonds!'

'Life advice from Savannah,' teased Brad, 'this is what my life was has come to!'

'What do you say, boss?' asked Andrew, looking eagerly at his director.

Brad checked his clipboard and call sheet. 'Stuart!' he yelled.

The runner instantly appeared by his side.

'I need legal approvals from four agents asap.

We'll have lost a few hours but we can make that up if we pull together.'

Brad clapped Andrew on the back. 'We might be going down but it won't be without a fight!'

CHAPTER SIXTEEN

IT WASN'T LONG BEFORE THE actors realised they had signed up for more than they'd bargained for. With no Gerri around, it meant they needed to do all the grunt work, including grooming and saddling their own horses. As they were on location and thus with a smaller crew, all departments were stretched thin.

'I never realised how much muscle Gerri put into making Arrow's coat shine,' moaned Savannah, as she brushed a dirty patch on Arrow's flank. 'My arm is killing me!'

'Tell me about it,' grunted Taylor. 'I think Sunny rolled in mud last night just to test me!' Clouds of dust flew into the air in bursts as Taylor attempted to brush the dry, caked mud out of her horse's hair.

Savannah stood back to survey her work. 'What do you think?' she asked the others.

Andrew paused and looked over. 'Not good enough,' he said with a smile. 'Come on, Savannah, you need to build up those muscles anyway!'

Savannah groaned again and got back to work.

'You're very chipper,' said Taylor, looking over at Andrew.

'I used to do this every weekend,' he replied, as he strapped a saddle to Chestnut. 'It was my life.'

Savannah rolled her eyes and turned to Bindi. 'Andrew loves to tell us what a champion rider he was before *Riding High* and Hollywood whisked him away.'

'It's all true,' said Andrew with a grin, as he expertly mounted his horse to prove his point. 'I miss it, if you must know.'

'You could still compete and do the show, couldn't you?' asked Bindi.

'Especially if you got a few early nights,' muttered Savannah.

'Maybe you're right,' said Andrew. 'In the

meantime, you guys better hurry up! We're meant to be on set in fifteen minutes!'

With a gentle squeeze on the reins, Andrew and Chestnut performed a perfect pirouette. 'See?' he said over his shoulder, as they trotted away. 'I haven't lost my touch!'

'That boy is maddening!' complained Savannah, as she rubbed at the sore patches on her hands where blisters were forming.

'Maddening but also lovely!' exclaimed Taylor, and promptly burst into tears.

'What's wrong?' asked Bindi, dropping her brush and walking over to Taylor. She put an arm around her shoulder.

'I've messed it all up,' gulped Taylor, as she wiped at the tears in her eyes.

'You'll ruin your make-up,' warned Savannah.

Taylor threw her a look.

'I'm just saying,' Savannah said softly, taking Taylor by the hand, 'you really need to start using waterproof mascara.'

'He's hated me ever since we broke up,' whispered Taylor.

'Actually, he doesn't,' said Bindi.

Taylor looked at her with surprise. 'How do you know?'

'He told me,' said Bindi. 'I have a feeling that you just have to say the word and you and Andrew will get back together.'

'Really?' asked Taylor, in disbelief.

'Really,' smiled Bindi.

'Yada, yada, yada,' Savannah gestured impatiently. 'This is no time for a group hug, guys!'

'But you'll have one anyway,' said Taylor, pulling Savannah in for a cuddle. The three friends giggled as they held each other in a long group hug.

Finally, Savannah pulled away and scrutinised Taylor's face. After much tut-tutting, Savannah pulled out her own cosmetics bag and began to work away at Taylor's ruined make-up.

Bindi threw a saddle on Jude's back and, once he was ready, moved on to help saddle Arrow and Sunny at lightning speed.

With two minutes to get to set, they were just going to make it!

CHAPTER SEVENTEEN

THE FIRST SCENE TO BE SHOT

involved completing a series of cross-country jumps. Andrew's character, Dean, was to be in the lead until his horse baulks at one of the jumps, nearly throwing Dean to the ground. With the cameras rolling, Andrew negotiated the course with ease and managed to make the stunt look completely believable in only one take.

'He really is good!' breathed Taylor, as she and the others watched from the sidelines.

'He's a one-take wonder,' said Savannah, not without admiration.

'He makes it look so easy,' said Bindi, starting to get butterflies again.

'Come on, girls!' called Brad. 'You're up!'

Brad explained the next shot. The three girls needed to complete the same course as Andrew. They would jump one behind the other to make it look like they were racing each other. Concerned for their safety, Brad instructed them not to go too fast but to keep their horses at a pace that they felt most comfortable with.

'And . . . action!' cried Lou, once everyone was in place.

Taylor was to ride first. Sunny took off at a dignified canter and they completed the three-jump course without incident. Bindi was next. As she approached the jump, it seemed so much bigger than it had from where they had discussed the shot. The jump consisted of a wooden gate constructed from solid timber planks.

'There's nowhere else to go but over!' Bindi sang to herself, trying to push her nerves away. She gave Jude an encouraging squeeze with her thighs. He took the hint and soared over the wooden structure with ease. After that, Bindi felt completely confident tackling the remaining jumps.

'Nice work,' said Andrew, as she drew up

alongside him. They both turned to watch Savannah approach.

Savannah was to bring up the rear. Her character, Cindy, was jealous of Eden and frantic to overtake her. This meant that Savannah really did need to ride faster than the others. On cue, she urged Arrow into a canter with a long lead-up to the jump. As she felt the rhythm of the horse, she urged him to go faster and his gait changed subtly from a canter to a slow gallop.

Savannah felt the rush of the air on her face and the adrenaline surging through her body as she moved towards the jump at such speed. She felt the moment of take-off and shifted her body weight forward to help Arrow over the jump. She had no idea how it happened but just as she felt the ground connect with her horse's hooves, she was suddenly freefalling. All too soon she fell to the ground with a thud. She felt Arrow's hooves whisk past her face, followed by the sound of him galloping away.

'No!' screamed Taylor, as she saw Savannah's body crumple to the ground.

'Quick!' yelled Brad. He motioned for first aid and sprinted towards Savannah.

Bindi and Taylor got there first. Taylor leapt off her horse, threw her reins to Bindi and crouched down next to Savannah.

'Savannah?' Taylor asked, as her hand hesitantly touched Savannah's shoulder. 'Can you hear me?'

There was an awful pause when nobody dared to speak. It felt like minutes until Savannah shifted slightly and coughed into the dirt. She sat up slowly, her face and hair brown with dust.

'I hope Gerri is paid well to do her job,' she said with a grimace and rubbed her left shoulder.

'Are you okay?' asked Bindi, kneeling down on the ground beside her.

Savannah nodded and stretched her neck on both sides. 'I think so.'

She tried to stand with Bindi's help but Brad insisted she remain still until the first-aid officer arrived.

'I'm fine!' Savannah grumbled. 'I have fallen off a horse more times than I can remember! Stop your fussing.'

'Are you sure?' asked Brad, looking at Savannah, doubtfully.

'That's life on a farm,' she said, brushing herself down and giving her limbs a good shake. 'No broken bones, see?'

Just then Savannah noticed a tear in her riding jacket which, Bindi noticed with amusement, seemed to cause Savannah more angst than the fall. 'This is vintage velvet,' she grimaced, examining the material.

'Maybe we should quit while we're ahead,' Brad suggested.

'Have designer clothing ruined for no reason?' Savannah pulled off the jacket. 'I don't think so.' She handed her jacket to Brad. 'You should keep the shot, it makes my character seem even more desperate to win. Come on, we've got no time to waste, let's keep moving, team!'

Andrew joined them with Arrow in tow. Savannah took the reins and remounted her horse. With a nod to Andrew, she rode off.

'Is that the same Savannah we've been

working with for three years?' asked a bewildered Andrew.

Brad nodded thoughtfully. 'I'm not sure and I don't care if aliens came to earth and swapped Savannah with new Savannah. She's a keeper!'

By the end of the day, everyone was completely physically and mentally exhausted. Their bodies weren't used to being in the saddle all day.

As they rode up to the stables at dusk, everyone was thinking about the same thing – a nice hot bath and a hearty meal!

Savannah tied her horse up to the post and began to make her way to the car that would take them to their hotel for the night.

'Uh, Savannah?' called Stuart. 'You can't go yet.'

Savannah stopped in mid-step and turned. She was so tired she could hardly see straight. 'Does Brad have notes to give us?'

Stuart shook his head. 'No, he's really pleased with the rushes. It's the horses – they need to be rubbed down, fed, and put away for the night. Then you can call it a day.'

Savannah wasn't sure if she saw the hint of a smile on Stuart's face. It was hard to tell in the dim light. Anyway, she was too tired to argue. She nodded mutely and trudged back to work.

CHAPTER EIGHTEEN

BY THEIR SECOND DAY ON location, the cast had adapted to their new responsibilities and a feeling of camaraderie had struck' up among them. The jibes and nastiness that had become the norm were gone and a warm friendship replaced it.

Andrew was relishing getting to do some real riding and had really impressed Brad with how adept he was in the saddle. He was getting to bed early, sleeping soundly and felt sharp and in control. His scenes had a new edge to them and he was no longer making silly mistakes on set.

It wasn't only Andrew who was changing.

After two days of shooting, Savannah showed the others the blisters on her hands, but instead of complaining, she was proud of them. It meant she couldn't wear her huge ring anymore but she didn't seem to care.

After lunch, Savannah and Bindi walked to make-up together, as they were both in the first scene for the afternoon. Bindi noticed Savannah was wearing less make-up and thought it really suited her.

'I have a confession to make,' Savannah said sheepishly.

'Uh-huh?' Bindi arched an eyebrow. 'Spill.'

'Jackson St has a store on Rodeo Drive but I didn't take you there the other day.' Savannah shrugged. 'I didn't want to have another big argument about animal rights.'

'O-kay,' said Bindi, a little hurt by Savannah's attitude.

'I wanted to apologise,' Savannah said, shooting Bindi a quick glance, 'for judging you like that.'

'That's okay,' said Bindi. As unlikely as their friendship might be, Bindi had begun to think of Savannah as a friend.

'Anyway,' Savannah continued quickly, 'I went there after you headed back to your hotel. I was so ready to spend up big but then I saw their window display. It was disgusting!'

'Why?' Bindi was surprised to hear Savannah saying anything negative about Jackson St.

Savannah pulled a face. 'It was like a safari scene with all the mannequins dressed in khaki uniforms and holding rifles. They had *real* stuffed animals – a snake coiled around the snakeskin bag, and a leopard. I mean, a real was-once-alive-but-now-not-so-much leopard.'

Bindi nodded. She could feel her hackles rise at the image Savannah was painting. 'And?'

'There was something about the glass eyes of the leopard, the deadness of them. I suddenly got it. Don't you see? The khaki, the bigger picture, it made my skin crawl . . .' Savannah bit a fingernail which was still colourful but now cut to a more practical length. 'So I took the bag back.' She looked up at Bindi to gauge her response.

'No way!' Bindi was surprised and pleased at Savannah's change in attitude.

Savannah smirked. 'I made a bit of a scene, now that I come to think of it. I marched right in and demanded to speak to the manager.'

'And?' gasped Bindi, wishing she'd been there to see it for herself.

'I threatened to expose them and withdraw my support if they didn't change their practices,' Savannah blurted out, relishing the memory.

Bindi stared at her co-star, incredulous.

Savannah smiled. 'It's a start, right?'

'It's brilliant!' Bindi exclaimed.

'You reminded me of something,' said Savannah. 'Fashion should be an expression of your personality. It should be fun and it should make you feel good. How can anyone feel good when they're wearing something that has hurt or killed wildlife, not to mention helped to wipe out an entire species?'

'Way to go!' Bindi couldn't hide her delight. 'Savannah Atwood – Wildlife Warrior!'

Savannah laughed. 'You realise you've created a monster, right?'

Bindi nodded. 'Yeah, but you're my kind of monster now!'

CHAPTER NINETEEN

AFTER FOUR LONG DAYS ON location, everyone was ready to head back to the studio. Bindi had mixed feelings about her week coming to an end. She was excited about finally being able to spend some time with Robert and her mum but was sad to leave her new friends.

The cast returned to find Gerri waiting for them in the stables. Taylor gave her a big hug.

'Are you okay, Gerri?' Taylor asked with concern. 'We were really worried about you, and Stuart said we couldn't visit you in the hospital.'

Gerri hugged her back with real affection. 'Thank you, I'm fine. Nothing a few days' rest can't cure.' She gave Bindi a quick glance, then turned to Andrew and Savannah. 'I've been hearing rumours that you two are putting me out of a job!'

Savannah blushed. 'There are going to be some changes made around here but I have a feeling you'll like them.'

Andrew pulled out a notebook filled with scribbles and rough illustrations. He opened it to show Gerri. 'I've had a few ideas for stunts we could try and I was wondering if you'd like to talk about them sometime.'

Gerri stared at the three kids she thought she knew so well. 'I don't know what was in the water on location but keep drinking it!'

As they set about unloading their gear and settling the horses, Stuart raced in. 'Brad wants to see all of you for an emergency meeting before you leave for the weekend,' he announced, struggling to catch his breath.

Andrew's eyes met Taylor's. 'He would have had the meeting with the network by now. It's crunch time. They must have decided to axe us,' he said grimly.

'We don't know that for sure,' said Gerri. 'Come on, let's go face the music.'

They made their way up to Brad's office and

waited outside his door. Bindi remembered sitting in the same spot five days before and thought how long ago it all seemed. Brad was still on the phone but they could hear strands of the conversation.

'I see. Well, thanks, Tim. I guess I better pass on the news.' He hung up the phone and opened the door of his trailer. The others waited to hear the news with bated breath.

Brad broke into a big smile. 'The network has decided to give us another season!' he exclaimed, throwing his hands in the air. Then he jumped down and high-fived Andrew and caught Taylor and Savannah in a bear hug.

'I don't believe it!' squealed Taylor.

'They loved the new scenes and how the action just jumps off the screen. They want more of this kind of fresh look to the show. "Like it was in the beginning", quote, unquote,' he said, making quote gestures with his fingers.

Brad looked Gerri up and down. 'You're looking very well for someone who has just had a stint in hospital. It's good to see you up and about,' he said, with a twinkle in his eye.

'It turns out the injury wasn't as bad as they first thought,' said Gerri, returning his smile.

'Excellent news because we have lots of work to do!' Brad gestured for Gerri to join him in his office.

'So much for a rest,' groaned Gerri, good naturedly. She held out her hand to Bindi and they shook. 'I like your work, Bindi Irwin.'

Bindi smiled, 'Back at ya, Gerri. Stay in touch.'

'I will!' Gerri gave her a wave and disappeared inside Brad's trailer.

Andrew, Savannah and Taylor were on cloud nine.

'We have to celebrate!' said Andrew.

'I'm not going to some dodgy party,' warned Savannah.

'I meant dinner or something,' said Andrew, with a sidelong glance at Taylor.

'I've got a better idea,' said Bindi. She pulled a flyer out of her bag. 'There's an opening tonight for a new ethical fashion label called Harvest. My mum was given tickets because of the work we do.'

Taylor took the flyer and looked at it. 'Sounds like fun,' she agreed, with a smile.

Savannah looked at Bindi suspiciously. 'Will I have to wear khaki?' she asked.

'You can wear whatever you feel like,' laughed Bindi. 'I'll be wearing a new dress!'

Savannah was instantly interested. 'Is that right? Bindi Irwin in a dress – this I have to see!'

They linked arms and walked off as Savannah pressed Bindi for details about the cut, the fabric and the label of her dress.

Andrew and Taylor were left alone together. After an awkward silence, Andrew cleared his throat then looked at Taylor meaningfully. 'A fashion opening sounds like it'll be girly. Maybe you guys should go without me?'

Taylor nodded. 'It will be girly and probably not at all your scene.'

'I get it, okay?' Andrew held up a hand to silence her. 'You girls have fun.'

'If you can get past the girliness,' Taylor continued quickly, 'I'd really like you to come as my date.' The words tumbled out in a rush and Taylor blushed.

Andrew held her gaze in disbelief. Then he broke into a big smile and his answer was written all over his face.

CHAPTER TWENTY

BINDI WAS STOKED TO BE HAVING

a night out with her mum and Robert. She had seen
very little of them over the course of the week and it
was exciting to get dressed up and hit the town.

'You look gorgeous, honey,' said Terri as they
stepped out of their taxi.

Robert cocked his head with a cheeky smile. Terri laughed, getting the hint, and added, 'And you look very handsome, Robert. It's a privilege to step out with you both.'

Robert nodded, satisfied.

'Shall we go in?' asked Terri, as she linked arms with her two children.

'You betcha!' cried Bindi and Robert in unison.

Harvest used natural fibres and organic processes in creating their range. They were proud to be 100 per cent environmentally sustainable. Their signature look involved colourful textures and weaves, and an eccentric use of layering, but somehow it all worked.

In stark contrast to their mother-earth message, they had chosen a venue which was raw and stark – the theme was earthy-meets-industrial-grunge!

The venue was an old warehouse they had transformed for the event.

Bindi felt as if she stood out like a sore thumb in her colourful pink and green floral dress, alongside LA's black-clad uber-trendy fashion elite. But she didn't care! With its A-line cut and full skirt, her dress might not have been 'on trend' but she felt really girly when she wore it – girly in a good way! She thought about what Savannah had said, that clothes should be an expression of how you feel. And she felt like celebrating!

The fashion parade wasn't a sit-down affair. People mingled amongst the models while finger food was passed around. Bindi, Robert and Terri were tucking into a satay tofu and haloumi slider drizzled in a fresh mint sauce, when Bindi noticed Taylor and Andrew arrive. They were holding hands.

'Over here!' Bindi yelled, waving until Taylor noticed her and motioned for Andrew to follow. After Bindi made the introductions, Andrew and Robert fell into conversation about male fashion. Andrew was surprised to hear that Robert had lots of strong opinions!

'You look very happy!' Bindi whispered to Taylor.

Taylor nodded, glowing. 'It's all good. *Really* good. I can't believe I let my mum get between us.'

Bindi squeezed her hand. 'It's good to see you happy.'

Taylor smiled and squeezed Bindi's hand in return. 'Thanks. I want you to promise you'll write to me. I'm going to miss you so much.'

Bindi nodded. She was going to miss them all too.

'Hey, Bindi,' Andrew shouted, in an effort to be heard over the pulsing music. 'I've decided I'm going to buy my own horse so I can get back into competing. Can you help me look for one?'

'I'd love to!' Bindi could think of nothing better. She and her family had a few more days in LA, and looking at horses was something she loved to do.

'When you think about it,' continued Andrew, 'if Gerri hadn't hurt herself, none of this would have happened.'

'Funny how things work out, isn't it?' mused Bindi.

Andrew smiled knowingly. 'I'm on to you, Bindi Irwin,' he whispered. Then he gave her a gentle nudge. 'Thanks.'

Bindi smiled. 'I have no idea what you're talking about.'

'Look!' exclaimed Taylor, pointing into the crowd. Savannah was making her way towards them. As always, she was hard to miss but this time it was for all the right reasons. She was dressed in an amazing floor-length dress which draped across her body in pastel shades of green and blue. The silk shone under the lights and she looked luminous.

'You look amazing!' said Andrew.

Savannah did a twirl to show her dress off to maximum effect.

'It's completely organic and hand-stitched and I love it! It makes me feel really . . . me!' she laughed at herself.

'You're glowing!' laughed Bindi.

'But wait,' said Savannah, 'there's more!' She held up the little purse she was carrying. 'Note my choice of handbag. No reptile was hurt in the making of this organic cotton purse.'

'Good for you!' said Taylor.

'I heard back from the head designer of Jackson St,' Savannah said, leaning closer to Bindi.

'And?' Bindi was eager to hear how the fashion house had responded.

'Well, they carried on for a bit at first but then we actually got talking and I shared some ideas I have for a few pieces, and they might even be interested in my designs!' exclaimed Savannah. 'Completely animal-friendly, of course.'

'You rock!' exclaimed Bindi, and gave her friend a high-five.

'In this dress?' said Savannah. 'I better!'

Just then, the media who were covering the event noticed Savannah and swarmed around her, shouting out questions and taking pictures. Gone was the guarded expression and the sceptical air Bindi had seen her wear in public. Savannah was in her element and she worked the crowd like a professional. She answered questions about Harvest, her dress, *Riding High* and her new-found commitment to ethical fashion. She happily posed for photo after photo, and looked as if she was thoroughly enjoying herself in her new role as animal ambassador.

Bindi was content to watch from the sidelines and take it all in. The week had been successful from a work point of view but she drew just as much joy from giving her new friends a helping hand.

Keep a lookout for the next two books in the

Bindi Behind the Scenes series

BOUNCING OFF THE MENU

and

A GHOSTLY TALE

Publishing October 2012